The Collected Tales of Little Mouse

A treasury of five delightful stories

Pictures by Caroline Anstey

PIPPBROOK BOOKS

Contents

Goodnight,
Little Mouse

Merry Christmas,
Little Mouse

Say Hello,
Little Mouse

Little Mouse, I Love You

O nce upon a time
there was a little mouse
who was always asking questions.
Luckily, she had a gran
who was always answering them,
and between them they made quite a pair.

"Gran," asked Little Mouse one day,
"what is love?"
"Love?" laughed Gran.
"Oh, that's easy, Little Mouse!
Come for a walk and you'll soon see!"

Gran and Little Mouse set off
through the garden where Grandpa
was digging his vegetable patch.
"Shh," hushed Grandpa,
and pointed to where a mother wren
was teaching her chicks how to fly.

"Just like the way you and Gran
show me how to do things!"
whispered Little Mouse.

Beyond the garden gate lay
the wood, and it wasn't long before
Little Mouse spotted a mother squirrel
digging up some of the acorns
she had hidden in the autumn,
and sharing them among her children.

"Just like the way you share
the food you've cooked with me!"
exclaimed Little Mouse.

Passing through the wood
they reached the meadow.
Little Mouse liked it there because she
could watch all the rabbits scampering
about outside their burrows.
But today, one little rabbit
had cut his paw on a sharp stone
and a mother rabbit was lying beside
him to keep him company
while he got better.

"Just like the way
you sit by my bed with me
if I'm feeling poorly,"
cried Little Mouse.

There was a field near the
meadow, and Little Mouse
caught sight of a lamb who
was running up and down, looking
very frightened of a sheepdog.
But just then, a mother sheep strode
out of the flock and went over to the lamb,
who looked much happier as he nuzzled up to her.
"You see," smiled Gran, "that mother sheep was
just telling the lamb not to worry about the
sheepdog. He is there to look after them."

"Just like the way you
tell me not to worry
when I feel frightened,"
said Little Mouse.

When they had passed by the field,
Gran and Little Mouse came to the
duck pond, where there was a lot of quacking
and splashing as a brood of baby ducklings
scrambled after their mother.
"Those ducklings will grow up one day,
won't they?" said Little Mouse.

"Do you think their mummy will forget them
when she has new ones to look after?"
"No," said Gran. "She will
never forget a single one!"

"Just like the way you will
never forget me!" said Little Mouse.

By now it was beginning to get dark and,
as Gran and Little Mouse turned to go home,
they passed a barn. They could hear hooting
coming from inside, so Little Mouse peeped
around the door to see a mother owl
giving her little ones a tender peck before
she set out for the night.

"Just like the way you give me a
bedtime kiss," whispered Little Mouse.
"Yes," agreed Gran. "Although for the owls
it's a good morning one!"
And they both laughed.

Now that the evening had come,
Gran and Little Mouse walked home quickly and
they soon saw Grandpa, waving at the gate.

"Gran," said Little Mouse.
"All of those things I saw today – sort of
added together – do they make up love?"
"You know," said Gran, "I really think they do."

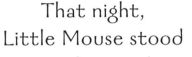

That night,
Little Mouse stood
at the window with Gran,
thinking about all the things she had seen.
"That was a lovely day,"
whispered Little Mouse.
"I do love you, Gran, and Grandpa, too."

"And I love you, Little Mouse," said Gran.
And with that, Little Mouse
gave Gran a goodnight kiss,
and tiptoed off to bed.

Thank You,
Little Mouse

Little Mouse loved staying
with Gran and Grandpa.
They were always so kind to her,
and every day she spent with them was
full of wonderful surprises.
Sometimes when Little Mouse went
out into the garden, Grandpa might
surprise her with some tasty treats from
his vegetable patch. And sometimes he
would play ball with her in the garden.

When Little Mouse went into the kitchen Gran
would suddenly present her with a tray of delicious biscuits,
or perhaps a lovely cake she had baked in secret.

And every evening she was sure
to read Little Mouse an extra-specially
nice bedtime story.

Of course, Little Mouse always remembered to say
'thank you', but Gran and Grandpa were so very kind to her
that saying 'thank you' just didn't always seem to be enough.

Each day Little Mouse would go for a
walk and, as the summer drew on and
turned into autumn, she noticed how the
vegetables were ripening in Grandpa's
vegetable patch, and how all
the nuts and fruits were ripening in
the fields and hedgerows.

Little Mouse could see the woodland animals
going here and there collecting their winter
store, and it gave her an idea.

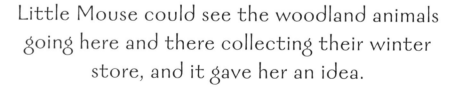

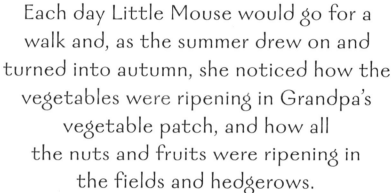

So Little Mouse borrowed
a wicker basket, and set off along
the woodland path until she came
across Little Squirrel, who had
been harvesting hazelnuts.

"If I help you to carry these
hazelnuts home, will you let me
have some?" she asked.
"Of course," said Little Squirrel.
And Little Mouse helped
carry the hazelnuts all the way
back to Little Squirrel's dray.

Next, Little Mouse met Little Rabbit,
who was looking lost under an apple tree.
"Can you help me, Little Mouse?"
said Little Rabbit. "I was searching for
fruit and I found all these apples, but
now I can't find my way home again."
"Of course," smiled Little Mouse, and she
helped Little Rabbit find her way home.
In return, Little Rabbit gave her
some big, juicy apples.

No sooner had Little Mouse said goodbye when she
came across Little Sparrow, who was sitting in
the middle of a blackberry bush. "Could I have
a few blackberries?" asked Little Mouse.

"Certainly," said Little Sparrow.
"But this bush is very thorny, and I seem to be stuck.
Can you help me find a way out?"

So Little Mouse helped Little Sparrow to get out of the middle of the thorny bush.

And Little Sparrow let her have some blackberries, and even one or two late strawberries that she had found.

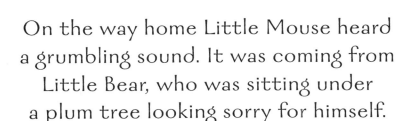

On the way home Little Mouse heard
a grumbling sound. It was coming from
Little Bear, who was sitting under
a plum tree looking sorry for himself.

"Can you help me, Little Mouse?"
he said. "I have a thorn stuck in my paw."
"Of course," said Little Mouse.
And with her teeth, Little Mouse had
soon taken out the thorn. Little Bear was
so grateful that he gave Little Mouse
some cherries and some plums.

By now Little Mouse's basket was full,
so she went back to Gran and
Grandpa's house, and hid everything
in her basket out of sight.

The next day Gran and Grandpa
went for a walk. They wondered why
Little Mouse didn't want to come
with them, but when they arrived
home again they had the surprise of
their lives. There was a big sign outside
of the garden gate that read:
LITTLE MOUSE'S
THANK YOU PARTY!

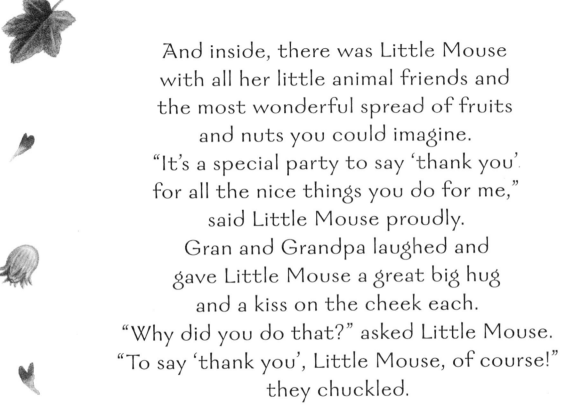

And inside, there was Little Mouse
with all her little animal friends and
the most wonderful spread of fruits
and nuts you could imagine.
"It's a special party to say 'thank you'
for all the nice things you do for me,"
said Little Mouse proudly.
Gran and Grandpa laughed and
gave Little Mouse a great big hug
and a kiss on the cheek each.
"Why did you do that?" asked Little Mouse.
"To say 'thank you', Little Mouse, of course!"
they chuckled.

AND EVERYONE LAUGHED.

Goodnight,
Little Mouse

It was time for Little Mouse
to go to bed and, after Grandpa
had read her a story, she wriggled
down under her snuggly quilt.
But no matter how she tossed and
tumbled or mumbled and grumbled,
she just couldn't get to sleep.
"Grandpa!" she called.
"I'm frightened!"

Grandpa came straight up to Little Mouse's
room to see what the matter was.
"I can't go to sleep, Grandpa!" said Little Mouse.
"It's dark and there are scary noises outside!"

"You needn't be afraid, Little Mouse!"
smiled Grandpa, giving her a cuddle. "The dark
can't hurt you! You are safe and snug in bed."
And with that, he went away again.

But just at that moment a gust of wind
must have blown outside for there came a loud
TAP TAP TAP
at the window. Little Mouse jumped.
"Grandpa!" she called.

Soon, Grandpa was at the door again.
"What's that tapping sound, Grandpa?"
asked Little Mouse.
So Grandpa took Little Mouse over
to the window, and showed her outside.
"Why!" said Little Mouse. "That tapping
sound was only the wind, blowing a
branch against the window!"

And just then, there was another sound.

It was a loud HOOT HOOT, far away.
Little Mouse looked very scared indeed!
"Don't you know what kind of bird hoots,
Little Mouse?" said Grandpa.

"Is it an owl?" asked Little Mouse.
"Yes!" exclaimed Grandpa. "Each night
Mother Owl leaves her nest to fly far
and wide over the countryside."
Just then there was another sound.

It was a BARK BARK BARK.
"I know that sound," cried
Little Mouse. "It's a dog!"
Noises didn't seem scary when
you knew what they were.

"No, Little Mouse,"
said Grandpa. "That isn't
a dog. Dogs sleep at night.
But foxes bark just like dogs.
Each night the fox leaves its den,
and sets off through the fields.
But you are safe, Little Mouse.
No foxes will come into the house."

"Let's listen and see if we can hear any other noises,"
said Little Mouse, and Grandpa agreed.
It didn't take long before
they heard a loud
SPLASH
from the stream
in the garden.

"Is that a bird?" said Little Mouse.
"Oh, no, Little Mouse," said Grandpa.
"Most birds sleep at night. That is an otter. Each night
he leaves his den, and dives into the stream for a swim."
Now, Little Mouse was starting to enjoy listening
for night sounds, but she did feel tired.
But she listened hard and heard a

patter patter patter

at the edge of the forest.
"Are they rabbits?" she asked,
giving out a big, sleepy yawn.

"Oh, no, Little Mouse,"
said Grandpa. "Rabbits curl up together
in their burrows at night. Those are another
night creature. They are badgers. If you
look hard you can see them, just at
the edge of the garden."

Little Mouse looked at the badgers,
then went back to bed. Now that she
knew what all the noises were she
didn't feel frightened any more.
"Thank you for coming to
see me, Grandpa!" she said.

Grandpa closed
the window and smiled.
"That's alright, Little Mouse," he said.
"I don't want you to be scared, so you will
always be safe and sound when I am close by."
But just as Grandpa leaned over to
hug Little Mouse and say, "Goodnight,"
what do you think he saw?

Why! Little Mouse was so tired, she was
fast asleep already, just as snug as a bug in a rug!
"Goodnight, Little Mouse!" said Grandpa. "Sleep tight!"
And do you know? That is exactly what
Little Mouse did, all night long!

Merry Christmas, Little Mouse

Little Mouse was getting ready
for Christmas. She hung up her
little stocking ready for Santa,
and wrapped up all her presents.
She was looking forward to seeing Gran
and Grandpa, who were going to visit on
Christmas Day. The only trouble was,
there wasn't any snow.
"I know it doesn't really matter,"
said Little Mouse to herself.
"But I'm still going to wish for snow."
And so she wished extra hard.

Then something magical happened.
First one snowflake fell,
then another, then another,
until the whole sky was filled with snowflakes.

Little Mouse was so excited she went out
into the garden and danced around and around
in the falling snowflakes.
Her friends Little Robin and Little Sparrow,
out hunting for winter berries,
fluttered around her as she danced.

And as Christmas Eve drew on, it snowed more and more...

By the evening there was such a lot of snow
that Little Mouse decided to stay indoors.
In fact, it had snowed so hard Little Mouse
started to wonder if Santa would be able
to get to their house that night.

"Of course Santa will come,"
laughed Ma Mouse.
"He has a magical sleigh that travels
along the ground, and flies over
the top of the trees and houses."
"But Gran and Grandpa can't fly!"
thought Little Mouse.

On Christmas Day, Little Mouse woke up early to find
Santa had delivered all her presents despite the snow.
But when she ran into the kitchen to wish Ma and
Pa Mouse a merry Christmas, she got a surprise.

To Little Mouse

There on the table was a card addressed,
"To Little Mouse", and in it she read:
"Merry Christmas, Little Mouse! We have gone to fetch
Gran and Grandpa. We will be home very soon!
Help yourself to a Christmas breakfast!
Love, Ma and Pa."

Little Mouse sat down to wait.
Outside, the world lay deep in snow,
and as time drew on she started to worry.
What if Ma and Pa Mouse were lost
in the snow? Little Mouse didn't like the idea
of spending Christmas alone in the house,
even if she did have Little Robin and
Little Sparrow for company.
But when she looked out into the garden,
even the two little birds had flown away!

Just then, she noticed something very strange.
There, in the snow, were two long tracks.
They must have been made by Santa's sleigh!
That gave her an idea...

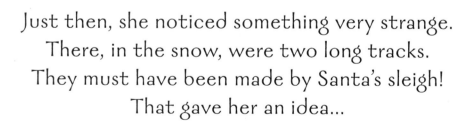

It looked as though Santa had
set off through the forest to Gran and
Grandpa's house. Little Mouse decided that she
would take her sledge and follow the tracks.
She would soon find Ma and
Pa Mouse and bring
them home!

At first the going was very easy – the tracks seemed
to be leading in the right direction. But then the snow became
deeper and the tracks disappeared. Santa's sleigh had flown away!
Little Mouse started to realise she might become
lost in the snow herself! Just as she was about
to turn and head for home, she noticed
something fluttering ahead of her.

It was Little Robin and Little Sparrow
and they had brought Little Fox with them,
and Little Squirrel, too!
"We thought the snow might be a bit deep
for you, Little Mouse!" they cried.
"So we went to see if Little Fox
might be able to help."

Soon Little Fox was pulling Little Mouse's
sledge homeward. And just around the next bend...

...they found Ma and Pa Mouse, and Gran and Grandpa Mouse, too! Little Mouse was so glad to see them, she ran up and gave them all the biggest Christmas hugs you can imagine. "I thought you had got lost in the snow," she said.

"And then I nearly
got lost myself,
but my forest friends
all came to help."

Ma Mouse invited all of Little Mouse's
friends to join them for Christmas dinner.
Little Mouse put on her special present
from Ma and Pa – a beautiful red dress
to match her Christmas hat.

"I am so glad you could come for Christmas,"
said Little Mouse to Gran and Grandpa.
"Spending Christmas with your family and friends
is the best present anyone can have!"
And Gran and Grandpa smiled big smiles and said,
"Merry Christmas, Little Mouse!"

Say Hello,
Little Mouse

Everyone was busy in
Little Mouse's house. Gran was making
lots of party food and the kitchen
was full of tasty baking smells.
"Gran," said Little Mouse,
"can we read one of my storybooks?"
"Sorry, Little Mouse," said Gran,
giving her a quick hug.
"I'm just too busy today.
But I think Grandpa will need your help –
why don't you go upstairs and ask him?"

In the littlest bedroom, Grandpa was busy
painting the walls a beautiful sky-blue colour.
"Just the mouse I need," said Grandpa.
"Come and help me with the finishing touches."
Little Mouse got her very own brush and special gold paint.
Together they covered the ceiling with stars of all sizes.
"A starry sky!" exclaimed Little Mouse happily.
"Just like in my room."

"That's right,"
replied Grandpa, smiling.
"Pa Mouse and I put
those stars on your ceiling
just before you were born."

Next, Little Mouse and Grandpa
went up into the cobwebby loft.
Right at the back, she helped Grandpa
to dust off a cot.
"That's a tiny bed!" said Little Mouse.
"This cot used to be yours," explained Grandpa.
Little Mouse didn't think it could ever
have been her bed. It was far too small –
she could never fit in there!

Back downstairs,
Gran invited Little Mouse
to go on a walk. Leaving the cakes to cool,
they set off into the wood.
"We have some special errands to run,"
Gran told her.
Deep in the woods, they knocked on Squirrel's door.
"Good afternoon, Grandma Mouse,"
said Squirrel.
"I found exactly what you were looking for."

Squirrel ran up her tree and brought back
a beautiful bath made out of an acorn cup.
"That's a tiny bath!" exclaimed Little Mouse. "Who could fit in there?"

Then Little Mouse
and Gran visited Little Sparrow.
"You have come at just the right time,"
said Little Sparrow. "I have just
finished your quilt, Grandma Mouse."
Little Sparrow brought out the
smallest quilt, filled with downy feathers.
What a tiny quilt, thought Little Mouse.
She took it very carefully and
folded it under her arm.

Back at the house, Gran and Grandpa
admired all their hard work.
The kitchen was full of tasty treats,
the hall was decorated with balloons and streamers,
and upstairs the smallest room looked lovely.

Little Robin came to help, flying right up to
the ceiling to put up their special sign.

What could it all be for, Little Mouse wondered?
"Ma and Pa are coming home," said Gran.
"And they're bringing a special surprise."

Finally everything was ready.
Little Rabbit arrived with a present – the most
teeny clothes Little Mouse had ever seen.
"Are you excited, Little Mouse?"
asked Little Rabbit, but Little Mouse
was too nervous to speak.

Suddenly, Ma and Pa walked in, carrying a tiny basket.
Little Mouse rushed over to them straight away.
"Say hello, Little Mouse. This is your baby brother."

Little Mouse looked down
at her brother. He was teeny and plump
with the smallest paws she had ever seen.
Little Mouse knew that she would have
to protect him and look after him
as he was so, so tiny.
Reaching behind her, Little Mouse
brought out a surprise of her own.
"This is Pink Rabbit," she whispered.
"He will look after you while you are asleep."

Ma and Pa were very proud of Little Mouse.
"Thank you, Little Mouse," said Pa.
"Your brother already loves you very much."
To show it, he had a new furry blue teddy for her!
Ma and Pa said that since she was going to be
his big sister, Little Mouse should choose her
brother's name. Little Mouse thought hard.
"I think the perfect name would be...
TINY MOUSE."
Everyone raised their cups.
"Welcome home, Tiny Mouse!"

PIPPBROOK BOOKS

First published as individual titles in the UK
between 2004 and 2008 by Templar Publishing
This anthology edition produced in 2013 by Pippbrook Books,
an imprint of The Templar Company Limited,
Deepdene Lodge, Deepdene Avenue, Dorking, Surrey, RH5 4AT, UK
www.templarco.co.uk

1 3 5 7 9 10 8 6 4 2

ISBN 978-1-84877-766-8

Designed by janie louise hunt and Manhar Chauhan
Written by Dugald Steer and Libby Hamilton
Edited by Liza Miller

Printed in China